The Cat and the Rooster

The Cat and The Rooster

A UKRAINIAN FOLKTALE

RETOLD BY *Ivan Malkovych*

PICTURES BY *Kost' Lavro*

Translated by Motria Onyschuk

Alfred A. Knopf   New York

THIS IS A BORZOI BOOK PUBLISHED BY ALFRED A. KNOPF, INC.

Translation copyright © 1995 by Motria Onyschuk
Text copyright © 1993 by Ivan Malkovych
Illustrations copyright © 1993 by Kost' Lavro

All rights reserved under International and Pan-American Copyright Conventions. Published in the United States of America
by Alfred A. Knopf, Inc., New York, and simultaneously in Canada by Random House of Canada Limited, Toronto.
Distributed by Random House, Inc., New York. Originally published in Ukraine by A-BA-BA-HA-LA-MA-HA Publishing
Company, Kiev, in 1993.

Manufactured in Singapore   10 9 8 7 6 5 4 3 2 1

Library of Congress Cataloging-in-Publication Data
Malkovych, Ivan.
The cat and the rooster / retold by Ivan Malkovych ; illustrated by Kost' Lavro ; translated by Motria Onyschuk.
p. cm.
Summary: When he does not follow the warnings of his friend the cat, a rooster is captured by a wily fox.
ISBN 0-679-86964-6 (trade)   ISBN 0-679-96964-0 (lib. bdg.)
[1. Folklore—Ukraine.]   I. Onyschuk, Motria. II. Lavro, Kost', ill. III. Title.
PZ8.1.M294Cat 1995
398.2'094704528617—dc20   94-14505   [E]

The Cat and the Rooster

O*nce upon a time,* there was a cat and a rooster, and they were great friends. The cat sang and played the fiddle, while the rooster only sang.

Every day the cat hunted for food, and the rooster stayed home to watch the house. Each time the cat went out, he warned the rooster:

"Don't let anyone in and don't go out, even if someone were to shout."

"Yes, yes," the rooster always said.

Then he would lock the door and wait for the cat's return.

One morning a hungry fox happened to see the cat leave, and she decided to try and trick the rooster. She crept up to the window and called:

"Come out, oh, rooster, please come out!
I have golden wheat for you to eat."

But the rooster replied:

"Cock-a-doodle-doo!
Cock-a-doodle-doo!
The cat has told me what to do!"

Seeing that this trick wouldn't work, the fox decided to come back that night. She scattered more golden wheat under the rooster's window and hid behind a bush.

The next morning, after the cat left, the rooster looked outside. He saw no one nearby and the golden wheat lying on the ground. The rooster thought:

"I'll go and eat a little wheat.
No one's about, no one will see, and no one will
tell the cat on me."

The rooster had just stepped outside when the fox jumped out from behind the bush, grabbed him, and ran off toward her home. The rooster crowed:

"Oh, help, brother cat! I don't know what to do!
The fox caught me when I didn't listen to you!
Cock-a-doodle-doo! Cock-a-doodle-doo!
Where are you? Oh, where are you?"

Deep in the woods, the cat heard the rooster's cry. But it was too late. He ran and ran, but he couldn't catch the fox. So the poor cat went home and cried.

Then he had an idea. He picked up his fiddle
and a sack, and he set off for the fox's house.

Meanwhile, the fox took the rooster home and tied him up in the pantry. Before she went off hunting again, she told her three daughters and son to watch the rooster and to keep the water hot so that once she returned, they could cook him.

"Be careful," she warned her children. *"Let no one in!"*

And then she left.

As soon as she was gone, the cat crept up to the fox's house. Seating himself outside the window, he began to play the fiddle and sing:

"Oh, the fox, oh, the fox,
She has a new house,
Three daughters and a son,
Two geese and a mouse.
Come out, foxes, look and see
How sweetly I can play."

The eldest daughter became curious and told the younger ones:

"You sit here, and I'll go see who's playing
and singing so sweetly."

She had just stepped out when the cat hit her on her head—smack!—and shoved her in the sack. He was so quick that the other foxes didn't see a thing.

Again the cat began to play his fiddle and sing:

"Oh, the fox, oh, the fox,
She has a new house,
Three daughters and a son,
Two geese and a mouse.
Come out, foxes, look and see
How sweetly I can play."

Now the second eldest daughter became curious. When she came out, the cat hit her on her head— smack!—and shoved her into the sack. In this way, the cat lured out all of the fox's daughters.

The fox's son waited for his sisters, but they did not return.

"I'll go outside and and tell them not to roam, so Mother won't scold us when she gets home,"
he said to himself.

He too left the house, and the cat hit him on his head—smack!—and shoved him into the sack.

Then the cat hung the sack high on a tree, went into the fox's house, found the rooster, and untied him. They ate all the fox's food, broke all her cups and bowls, and ran away home. From then on, the rooster always listened to the cat, and they lived happily ever after.

IVAN MALKOVYCH was born in the Carpathian Mountains. He is a poet whose work has been published in Ukraine. He lives in Kiev, where he is the founder and director of the A-BA-BA-HA-LA-MA-HA publishing house.

KOST' LAVRO was born in 1961 near Kiev, Ukraine. He is a graduate of the Kiev Academy of Art and has worked as an illustrator for several leading Ukrainian publishers and magazines. He has illustrated more than a dozen books for children and adults, and has won awards in three national graphic exhibitions. He lives in Kiev.